Copyright © 2019 by Drew Brockington • Cover design by Jen Keenan. • Cover copyright © 2019 by Hachette Book Group, Inc. • Hachette Book Group supports the right to free expression and the value of copyright. The purpose of copyright is to encourage writers and artists to produce the creative works that enrich our culture. • The scanning, uploading, and distribution of this book without permission is a theft of the author's intellectual property. If you would like permission to use material from the book (other than for review purposes), please contact permissions@hbgusa.com. Thank you for your support of the author's rights. • Little, Brown and Company, Hachette Book Group, 1290 Avenue of the Americas, New York, NY 10104 • Visit us at LBYR.com • First Edition: June 2019 • Little, Brown and Company is a division of Hachette Book Group, Inc. The Little, Brown name and logo are trademarks of Hachette Book Group, Inc. • The publisher is not responsible for websites (or their content) that are not owned by the publisher. • Library of Congress Cataloging-in-Publication Data • Names: Brockington, Drew, author, illustrator. • Title: Hangry / by Drew Brockington. • Description: First edition. | New York : Little, Brown and Company, 2018. | Summary: "A young monster takes the train into the big city, only to find his favorite hot dog vendor is closed and he's unable to satiate his hunger, leading to an epic case of destructive crankiness"— Provided by publisher • Identifiers: LCCN 2017044041 | ISBN 9780316559324 (hardcover) | ISBN 9780316559300 (ebook) | ISBN 9780316559379 (library edition ebook) • Subjects: | CYAC: Monsters—Fiction. | Hunger—Fiction. | Anger—Fiction. | Frankfurters—Fiction. • Classification: LCC PZ7.1.B7575 Han 2018 | DDC [E]—dc23 • LC record available at https://lccn.loc.gov/2017044041 • ISBNs: 978-0-316-55932-4 (hardcover), 978-0-316-55936-2 (ebook), 978-0-316-55930-0 (ebook), 978-0-316-55927-0 (ebook) • PRINTED IN CHINA • 1010 • 10 9 8 7 6 5 4 3 2 1

The illustrations for this book were created using mixed media. This book was edited by Russell Busse and designed by Jen Keenan. The production was supervised by Erika Schwartz, and the production editor was Annie McDonnell. The text was set in Chauncy, and the display type is hand lettered by Drew Brockington.

BURGER TIME

TACO TUESDAY

TACO TUESDAY

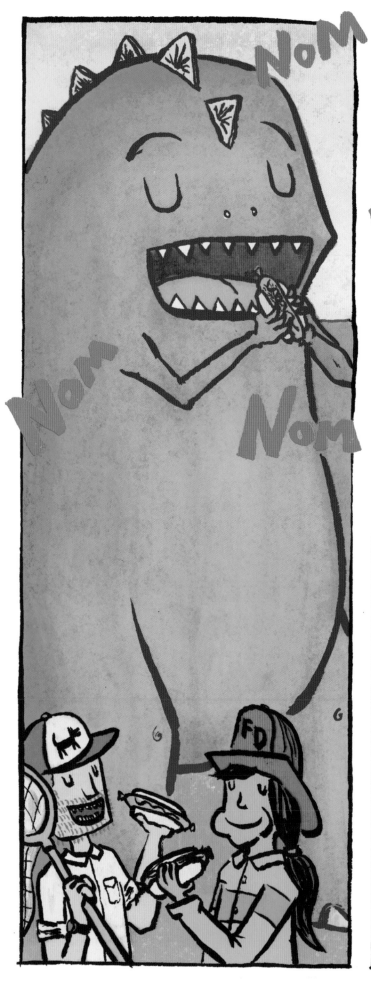